FRANKIE and FRIENDS
BREAKING NEWS

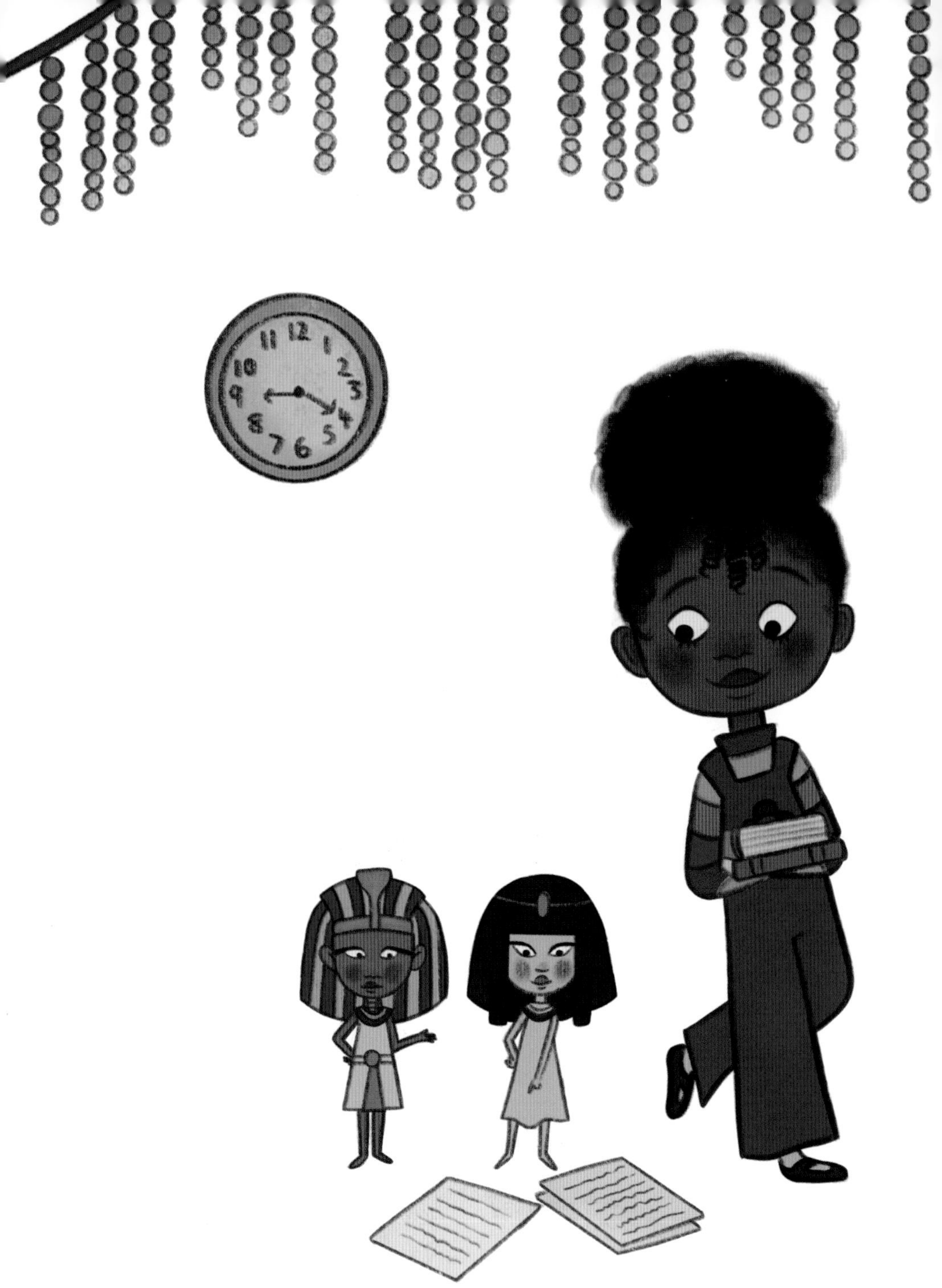

FRANKIE and FRIENDS
BREAKING NEWS

Christine Platt
illustrated by Alea Marley

WALKER BOOKS

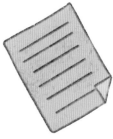

Text copyright © 2023 by Christine Platt
Illustrations copyright © 2023 by Alea Marley

First edition 2023

Library of Congress Catalog Card Number 2022922923
ISBN 978-1-5362-2209-8

23 24 25 26 27 28 CCP 10 9 8 7 6 5 4 3 2 1

Printed in Shenzhen, Guangdong, China

This book was typeset in Glypha LT Std.
The illustrations were created digitally.

Walker Books US
a division of
Candlewick Press
99 Dover Street
Somerville, Massachusetts 02144

www.walkerbooksus.com

For Alice Dunnigan,

the first Black woman journalist to earn

White House press credentials

CHAPTER ONE

Frankie sat on the floor in her parents' bedroom and watched as Mama finished packing the small suitcase she used when traveling for work. When Mama put her special press badge for journalists around her neck, Frankie knew she'd be leaving for the airport soon.

"I'm sorry I have to go," Mama said. "You know I hate to miss out on family card games. But whenever there's BREAKING NEWS, it's my job to cover the story."

"Like the breaking news you had to cover during the presidential election?" Frankie asked.

"Exactly," Mama said. "Breaking news is about something that's happening in the moment. It's information that people need to know right away."

Frankie sighed. Mama was the best and toughest journalist in the world, so of course Frankie was proud. She just wished breaking news would take a nap so that Mama could finish a game of Crazy Eights for once.

"We'll miss you, but we understand." Papa placed his hand on Mama's shoulder. "JOURNALISM is important work. We're not the only people who need you."

Frankie smiled. Papa always reminded

them that Mama's job helped hundreds

(and sometimes even thousands) of people

get the information they needed.

"Because everyone needs to know the news, right?" Frankie's older sister, Raven, started twisting her curls. Frankie watched her closely. Whenever Raven played with her hair, she was usually worried.

Frankie tried to lift her sister's spirits. "Yes, Mama, we'll miss you. But we know that the world of journalism needs you. So we'll stop playing Crazy Eights right now, and we won't play again until you're back home."

"Well, that's awfully nice of you." Mama playfully pinched Frankie's cheek. "I know how much you love that game. I promise I'll be home in a few days."

Just as they always did before Mama left to report on something important,

everyone gathered for a group hug. Papa,
Raven, and Frankie
all sang out,
"Mama's leaving so
we're singing the
blues. 'Cause
Mama's got to go
report breaking
news!"
 "Mama's got
to go! This much
is true. And while
I'm away, I'll be
thinking of you!"
Mama sang
back and gave
everyone a kiss.
 As Mama finished packing, Papa and

Raven left to do the things that papas and big sisters had to do. Maybe Papa would cook a delicious spaghetti dinner to make them feel better. Frankie loved slurping up noodles covered in his special pasta sauce.

Raven was probably going to call and text all her friends. Then they'd record silly videos together.

But Frankie wasn't leaving. She wanted to stay with Mama until the last second.

"Are you sure I can't come with you?" Frankie eyed Mama's suitcase as she sat on the floor. If she folded her arms and legs just right, Frankie was certain she could fit.

Mama zipped up her suitcase and put on her serious journalist glasses. She sat down on the floor across from Frankie and leaned in slowly until their foreheads touched and their eyes crossed. Frankie started giggling.

"I wish you could join me, Frankie," Mama said. "Do you remember what HARD NEWS is?"

One day, Frankie would be an award-winning journalist too, so she always listened closely when Mama talked about

work. Frankie pulled out the special journalist notepad she always kept in her back pocket and flipped to her notes. She couldn't wait to show Mama how serious she was about journalism.

"Yes!" Frankie replied. "Hard news is when something very serious is happening. Something that is so serious, only adults need to know about it."

"You've got it!" Mama smiled. "I'm so proud of you! And this assignment is hard news. So unfortunately, you can't come with me. We'll have to wait for another breaking news story, maybe something that's happening here in town. Something that's the perfect story for kids to know about too."

Sometimes Frankie went with Mama to the local news station, which was a lot of fun. Once she even got to sit behind the fancy news desk! Frankie had looked right into the television cameras and pretended to go live as she gave a news report, just like Mama.

"I can't wait until I grow up and I'm a famous journalist too." Frankie twisted her forehead against Mama's as they made silly faces. "Then I can come with you whenever you report on breaking news *and* hard news."

Mama smiled. "Me either! We'll report on all the news together."

"Can we report on human-interest stories too?" Frankie loved learning about ordinary people doing amazing things. Her favorite was the boy who found a stranger's wallet. Instead of taking the money and buying bags of candy, he took it to the police station. That boy got to wear a real police badge for a whole day.

Frankie was really impressed that he did the right thing. He didn't even ask for a reward! If Frankie had been there, she would have told him to ask for free ice cream for a year.

"Absolutely!" Mama said. "In fact, we'll be our own human-interest story: the best mother-daughter journalism team ever."

"I can't wait!" Frankie said excitedly. "We can call it *The Mama Franklynn and Frankie News Show!*"

Mama laughed and gave Frankie a big hug. "Until then, be on the lookout for developing stories at home. News is happening all around us all the time. Do you have the special press badge we made together?"

The last time Mama went overseas to cover a hard news story, she helped Frankie make a press badge so she could officially report on stories that happened in their community.

"Of course, Mama." Frankie tapped the *Citizens' Press* badge she often wore around her neck. "If there's any news that happens while you're away, I'll make sure to report on it."

"Perfect! Thank you for covering for me," Mama said. "Now, this is Franklynn McKnight, signing off to head to the airport to cover breaking news in another city."

Frankie smiled proudly. "And this is Frankie McKnight, signing off to cover news stories right here at home while Mama . . . uh, Franklynn McKnight is away." She pulled out her notepad and wrote *Breaking News at Home*, then underlined each word carefully. Frankie couldn't wait to find something to report on.

CITIZENS' PRESS

FRaNKiE

CHAPTER
TWO

The house always felt a little bit empty
after Mama left for work. Papa's office was
in the basement, so Frankie could watch
him working on his computer through the
glass doors whenever she wanted. It was
hard knowing that Mama was off working
but not being able to see her until she
appeared on television.

Frankie walked past Raven's bedroom
and heard her big sister laughing on the
phone with her friends. Raven used to keep

her bedroom door open so Frankie could stop by whenever she wanted. But ever since Raven became a teenager, her door was always closed. Now Frankie had to knock on Raven's door and wait for her to open it. And sometimes when Raven was doing "teenager stuff" she wouldn't even let Frankie inside!

Once Frankie got to her bedroom, she tried to cheer herself up by looking at the amazing journalist things Mama had given her. There was a cool voice recorder, although Mama said that a notepad and pen were a journalist's best friends. There was also the whiteboard that Mama once used to sketch out stories. And there were three things that Frankie loved the most: Mama's old video camera, an old microphone, and a real leather messenger bag to carry everything in.

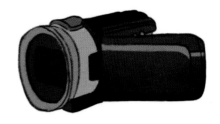

"Hey, I have an idea!" Frankie said.

"I have everything I need to make my own news studio!"

First, Frankie moved her desk and chair to the middle of her bedroom.

Next, she put Mama's old microphone on her desk. Then, she slid the whiteboard behind her chair and picked up her favorite green marker.

"*Frankie and Friends.*" She giggled as she wrote each word. "The best news show *ever!*"

Now all she needed was a news crew.

Frankie looked around her bedroom carefully. She picked up Farrah, her first doll and best friend. They'd spent their entire lives together and even looked alike! Farrah always knew exactly what Frankie was thinking.

"Mama says that she wouldn't be an award-winning journalist if it wasn't for her amazing team," Frankie reminded Farrah. "So are you ready to help me pick the perfect news crew?"

Farrah smiled. "Ready!"

"Who do you think would be best for sound and lighting?" Frankie asked.

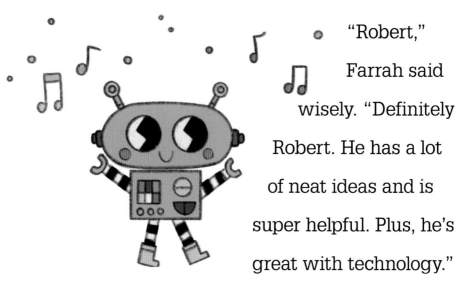

"Robert," Farrah said wisely. "Definitely Robert. He has a lot of neat ideas and is super helpful. Plus, he's great with technology."

Robert the robot whizzed over to the news desk, his lights blinking as he played a happy tune. "Whatever you need, I'm your guy!"

"What do you think about King Tut and Queen Cleopatra as copyeditors?" Frankie asked. "You know, to fact-check our stories and make sure everything is good to go?"

"Perfect choices," Farrah agreed. "They are well-traveled and very opinionated. Just the voices of reason that you need."

Queen Cleopatra and King Tut adjusted their golden crowns before strolling over to the news desk. When Mama had covered a news assignment in Egypt, she'd brought them back as special gifts for Frankie. The queen and king were very smart, but they rarely agreed on anything.

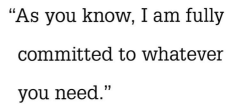

"Always happy to be of assistance," Queen Cleopatra said, bowing.

"As you know, I am fully committed to whatever you need."

"As I am." King Tut bowed deeper than Queen Cleopatra. "Not

that this is a competition in commitment. But if it were—"

Queen Cleopatra interrupted. "Let me guess. You think you would be the most committed." She shook her head in disbelief. As usual, the two royals began to argue.

Frankie laughed. "King Tut and Queen Cleopatra, you are both *equally* committed to whatever I need. And for that, I am grateful."

Frankie rubbed the top of her favorite teddy bear's head. "Dan, do you think you can handle operating the camera? You'll have to pay attention, though. You know how easily distracted you are."

Dan smiled proudly. "I won't let you down, Frankie!"

Frankie's orange-and-white tabby cat, Nina Simone, twirled around Frankie's legs and purred. "Of course you're part of the news crew, silly. I can't do anything without you!"

With her news crew assembled, Frankie clapped her hands. "All right, everyone. Family card games have been canceled. Mama had to leave to cover some breaking news."

Nina Simone frowned as she sang out

a large "Meow!" She wanted Frankie to know she'd miss Mama too.

"Nina, we all feel the same way," Farrah said. "That's why Frankie has set up this lovely news studio so we can report on our own news story!"

Frankie smiled. "That's right, Farrah. Welcome to the *Frankie and Friends* news studio! This is where award-winning journalist Frankie McKnight—me—will report on breaking news right here at home. And as my trusted news crew, you're going to help me make it all happen!"

The news crew was very excited. Dan plugged in the video camera so it could start charging while Robert flashed all his lights to make sure he didn't need any new bulbs. Queen Cleopatra and King Tut had a mini debate about the best way to check facts. Nina Simone licked her fur, carefully grooming herself to make sure she was camera-ready.

Frankie sat in her chair, kicked her feet up on the news desk, and cleared her throat. "OK, everyone. Gather around! It's time for our first huddle. We need to brainstorm.

"I want your OPINIONS on what my first news story should be about."

Everyone rushed over. Suddenly, Robert's eyes started flashing. He raised his shiny arms in the air and spun in circles like he always did when he got excited.

"Let's hear it, Robert." Frankie tapped her pen on her notepad like Mama did when she talked to the news crew at the local station.

"Not to make your first news show about me," Robert began.

"But imagine a report on the importance of robots. We're quite intelligent, you know."

Nina Simone let out another loud meow to voice her concerns. Because no one was more intelligent than cats. Not even humans!

"I believe you are leaving out an important bit of information," King Tut cautioned. "Robots are known as a form of artificial intelligence. As you know, or maybe you don't know, *artificial* means that you are a copy of something natural. So the humans who made you are therefore more intelligent than you."

Robert's lights flashed brightly. "I am *not* a copy—"

"All that being said," King Tut interrupted. "Robots could make for interesting news. Frankie could report on how everyone will need a robot in the future. Having subjects to rule over is important."

"Well, I—" Robert tried to defend himself.

"But will *everyone* need a robot in the future?" Queen Cleopatra asked. "We need an important story that interests everyone. Of course, this is not to say that *you* are not important, Robert . . ."

"Mama said news is happening all around us all the time," Frankie said. "Maybe—"

"Sorry to interrupt," Dan apologized, rubbing his furry ears. "Frankie, you said I need to focus. And I am trying, truly. But that sound . . . is someone crying?"

FRANKIE
and Friends

Everyone quieted. They too heard faint, muffled cries. Who was it? Or rather, *what* was it? And where was it coming from?

"I hear crying too!" Frankie whispered. "This is what Mama calls a DEVELOPING STORY. It's like a mystery. Something is happening, but you don't have all the facts

yet, so the story is still growing. And it's
our job to figure out what's going on!"

"Well, what are we waiting for?" Farrah
asked. "Let's solve it!"

"Yes," Dan agreed. "We have to
hurry before this developing story is fully
grown!"

CHAPTER
THREE

Frankie quickly walked over to her large

whiteboard and picked up a purple dry

erase marker. "All right, news crew,

the first thing we need to do with any

developing story is outline the BEATS."

Dan smiled fondly. "I remember when

you took me to one of your first violin

lessons. Your music teacher said, 'Stay on

beat, Frankie!'"

Robert's eyes blinked with excitement

as he twirled around Dan and played a funky beat.

"Oh yeah, oh yeah!" Dan wiggled and danced.

"Knock it off, guys," Farrah scolded. "This is serious news business."

"Yes, there are beats for music," Frankie explained. "But news beats are different." She gave Robert a stern look. He stopped playing music and listened. "In journalism, a beat is a subject or topic that is being reported on. Some stories have just one beat, like the opening of a bookstore."

"I love books!" Dan squealed.

"Shhhh!" The news crew hissed at Dan.

"Books are awesome!" Dan whispered.

Farrah raised her hand. "So even

though this is one developing story, there could be several parts to it? Several beats?"

"Exactly! So what's one beat that we know?" Frankie wrote *News Beats* on the whiteboard.

"Well, we know someone or some*thing* is crying," Dan said.

Nina Simone meowed in agreement. Then she lay on the floor and curled up to take a nap.

"Right!" Farrah agreed. "And we know

that whoever or whatever it is, it's probably in the house because we can hear it clearly."

Everyone quieted. And there again was the faint sound of crying. Dan went over to the window and listened, then shook his head to confirm the cries weren't coming from outside.

Frankie wrote *someone or something crying* on the whiteboard. "Can we think of any other beats? What happened before the crying began?"

"Mama left for work," Queen Cleopatra offered.

King Tut cleared his throat. "Actually,

Frankie's mama was
enjoying a game of cards
with her family when
she was suddenly
called upon to leave
for this troubling
thing adults call *work*."

"Well, adults *have* to go to work, right?"
Farrah reasoned. "It's how they make
money to buy important things like food
and toys and books."

"Actually, adults wouldn't have to go to
work if they just let robots do their jobs for
them," Robert chimed in.

"I like food and toys and books.
Especially food." Dan smiled and patted his
fluffy tummy.

Queen Cleopatra had had enough of the

chitchat. "Let's get back to focusing on the beats, shall we?"

"Right," Frankie said. "I think I need to go undercover for this developing story. It's the only way to find out *who* or *what* is crying."

"Why would you want to go under the covers?" Dan asked, confused, as he peeked under Frankie's quilt. "It's so dark! Being under the covers is only fun if you have a flashlight. Do you want me to get the one you took on your camping trip?"

Frankie sighed. "No, Dan. Not under the covers. Undercover. You know, like a detective."

Robert's eyes flashed as he played the theme song to *Mission: Impossible.* Dan dropped to the floor and sneakily crawled on his belly. Nina Simone swatted him away with a flick of her tail.

"I don't think it's safe to go undercover alone," Farrah reasoned. "I'm coming with you."

Frankie picked up Farrah and sat her on top of her shoulder so she could be lookout. "If you see something important, let me know!"

CHAPTER FOUR

When Frankie and Farrah stepped into the hallway, they realized the muffled cries were definitely coming from inside the house. And the crying was close by! Slowly and quietly, the two inched down the hallway. The closer they got to Raven's room, the louder the cries became.

Frankie and Farrah looked at each other in surprise.

"Is that—" Frankie whispered.

"Could it be?" Farrah whispered back.

Once they were outside Raven's bedroom, Frankie put her ear to the door. Then she held Farrah up so she could listen too.

Frankie pulled out her notepad and wrote *BEAT: Raven is crying! Unbelievable!*

"Let's get back to the news studio!" Farrah said quietly.

BEAT

Raven is crying!

Unbelievable!

When they got back, Frankie said to the news crew, "It's Raven! The crying is coming from her room." Frankie wrote *Raven is crying* on the whiteboard. Then she added, *Why?*

Frankie knew that people cried for different reasons. Mama said that sometimes people were so happy that tears of joy escaped their eyes. People also cried when they were sad. Frankie had definitely done that before. Sometimes, people even cried because they were angry.

Before Raven's thirteenth birthday, Frankie had cried with her big sister many times. At sad movies. Whenever they lost something they really loved. But now that

Raven was a teenager, they didn't do that kind of stuff together anymore. In fact, there were a lot of things they no longer did together. Frankie didn't even know that thirteen-year-olds cried!

Everyone tried to think of why Raven could be crying. But there were so many possibilities.

"You could ask her," Dan suggested. "I always ask questions when I want to know the answer to something. Besides, isn't that what journalists do? Especially when a story is developing?"

Everyone turned to look at Dan, surprised. Could he possibly know what he was talking about?

Nah!

"I don't know," Queen Cleopatra said. "Sometimes, people want to be left alone when they are crying."

"But sometimes, people want someone to ask them what's wrong," King Tut reasoned.

Frankie wasn't sure what to do next. Asking Raven why she was crying didn't seem like a good idea, especially now that she was a teenager. Frankie could pretend to know why Raven was crying as part of her news show. But that wouldn't be honest. And Mama always said that journalists had a responsibility to be honest, to only report on the FACTS.

"Not to make this about me," Robert said.

"But do you think Raven is crying because she wishes she had a robot?"

Nina Simone meowed in disagreement. Queen Cleopatra, King Tut, and Robert continued to argue about whether it was appropriate to ask someone about their sadness. Dan just smiled, distracted by a pretty blue bird sitting on Frankie's windowsill.

Frankie turned to Farrah. "You know me better than anyone," she whispered. "What do *you* think I should do?"

"I think you should ask Raven what's wrong," Farrah said wisely. "That's what a good sister—and journalist—would do. That's what Mama would do!"

"You're right." But Frankie was nervous. What if she knocked on the door and Raven wouldn't let her inside? What if Raven was dealing with "teenage stuff" and didn't want to be bothered by her little sister?

"Of course, you don't have to go alone." Farrah took Frankie's hand. "I'll go with you!"

"I'd like that very much," Frankie said. She hugged Farrah closely. Finding out why Raven was crying was not only breaking news; it was *hard news* too.

"All right everyone, quiet down," Farrah demanded. "This is Frankie's first breaking news story, and as her crew, we need to support her. After much consideration, she's going to INTERVIEW Raven."

Queen Cleopatra buried her face in her hands. "Oh dear! What if Raven just wants to cry in peace?"

"I think it's a great idea!" King Tut said encouragingly. "Risky, perhaps. But how else will you discover the truth?"

Frankie looked at her watch. It was already 4 p.m. She had less than an hour before

Frankie and Friends went live! If she was going to interview Raven and put a story together, there was no time to waste. Quickly, she took Farrah in her arms and they stepped into the hallway once again.

Mama had always told Frankie there were two types of questions that journalists asked during an interview: CLOSED-ENDED and OPEN-ENDED. As Frankie walked toward Raven's room, she thought about asking Raven closed-ended questions, because they were easier to answer. Raven would simply have to say "yes" or "no."

But Mama was a fan of open-ended questions. She always said, "I like to give people the chance to say what's in their hearts and on their minds."

As Farrah and Frankie stood outside Raven's bedroom door, the muffled cries grew louder.

"Are you ready?" Farrah asked Frankie.

Frankie took a deep breath. She had her best friend, her notepad, and her *Citizens' Press* badge. "I'm ready."

CHAPTER FIVE

Frankie knocked on Raven's bedroom door. The crying immediately stopped.

"Who is it?" Raven's voice cracked.

"It's me," Frankie said. "And Farrah. Can we come in?"

"Sure. Just . . . just give me a second."

When Raven opened the door, there were no tears on her face. But her eyes were red and swollen, just like someone who had been crying. "What's up, little sis?"

"Just be honest!" Farrah whispered. "Journalism is all about trust!"

"Raven, I heard you crying." Frankie stood as tall as she could in the doorway and took a deep breath before she asked her first open-ended question. "What's wrong?"

"Oh, Frankie, you wouldn't understand." Raven sniffled. "Being a teenager is hard."

"Well, not being a teenager is hard too," Frankie shared. "In fact, the only thing that's probably harder than not being a teenager is being an adult."

Raven smiled at Frankie.

"Or being a mouse," Farrah whispered. "That seems like a pretty hard life."

"Farrah thinks it's probably pretty hard being a mouse too," Frankie offered. "Can

you imagine having to break into people's
homes just to look for cheese?" She
shuddered. "Poor things!"

And then, much to Frankie's surprise,
Raven burst out laughing. "Little sister,
you are so silly!" She tickled Frankie (and
Farrah!) as she squeaked like a mouse,
"Give me some cheese! Now!"

Soon, everyone was laughing. Raven's eyes looked much better, and she was even smiling.

"Thanks for cheering me up." Raven gave her sister a big hug. "I was missing Mama in the worst way."

"Is that why you were crying?" Frankie asked. "And just so you know, I'm not being nosy." She tapped her *Citizens' Press* badge. "I need this information for my news show."

"*You* have a news show?" Raven asked, surprised. "Do tell!"

"Why don't you join us in the news studio?" Frankie suggested.

"Yeah!" Farrah said. "C'mon!"

"All right," Raven agreed. "But first let me answer your question, Frankie the journalist." She crouched down next to her little sister. "Yes, that's the reason I was crying. I miss Mama. But because I'm a teenager, I feel like I shouldn't cry about it."

Frankie gave her sister an encouraging hug. "Well, I think it's OK for everyone to cry. In fact, isn't crying a part of being human?" Frankie motioned for Raven to come closer so she could whisper in her ear. "I think crying is like pooping. Everyone has to do it at some point or another!"

Raven burst out laughing again. "Oh,

Frankie! I love you so much. Now, let's see this news studio of yours. I can't wait!"

Raven followed Frankie and Farrah back into the news studio. Raven sat on the floor and snuggled with Nina Simone while Dan set up the camera and Robert flashed his lights. Frankie took a seat at her news desk, feeling very much like an official journalist. Then, she pulled the microphone close and sat Farrah, her trusted co-anchor, beside it.

"Welcome to the *Frankie and Friends* news studio, Raven," Frankie said proudly as she leaned toward the microphone.

"It's amazing!" Raven picked up Frankie's pencil case and drawing paper. "I'll make a logo for you."

"Really?" Frankie was so excited. Raven was the best artist she knew.

Raven started drawing carefully.

"What's your TAGLINE?"

Frankie frowned. "What's that?"

"You know, a clever phrase about your show that people remember," Raven explained.

"Hmm, let me discuss this with the news crew." Everyone huddled together, and after a few minutes Frankie announced, "We've got it! *Frankie and Friends*. Tagline: Kids' news that you can use."

"It's perfect!" Raven added it to her drawing. "Ta-da! What you think?" She held up the *Frankie and Friends* news logo so everyone could see.

"I love it!" Frankie checked the time on her watch. They only had a few minutes left. "Quick! Raven, go get Papa so he can be here when I GO LIVE at five!"

Raven ran to get Papa.

"Oh my!" Papa smiled as he looked around Frankie's news studio. "This is amazing!"

Frankie smiled proudly. "Thank you, Papa. You're just in time for our first breaking news report."

Papa and Raven sat on Frankie's bed. They couldn't wait for *Frankie and Friends* to begin.

Dan went and stood behind the camera. Once he was certain that everything was working, he gave a thumbs-up. Robert flashed his green lights. Queen Cleopatra and King Tut waited next to the news desk, ready to help Frankie if she needed them.

"And you're on the air in five, four, three, two . . ." Farrah counted down. As soon as she said "one," she pointed at Frankie.

"Good evening,"

Frankie announced. "And thank you for joining me on *Frankie and Friends*. Today's breaking news is a heartwarming story about how two sisters learned to help each other through a difficult time."

"You're an excellent journalist!" Raven whispered.

"Sometimes, mamas have to go to work," Frankie said matter-of-factly. "And sometimes, when mamas leave, you might want to cry. Even big sisters! That's why it's important to check on each other and to ask the tough questions, even if you're scared. Today, two sisters discovered they're not alone in how they feel. And together, they created something special. This very news show, *Frankie and Friends*."

Once she had finished her introduction, Frankie interviewed Raven along with the entire news crew so they could share their thoughts.

Farrah spoke about the
importance of being brave.
Queen Cleopatra and

King Tut didn't disagree on a

single thing. And

Dan didn't get

distracted once!

There was even

a commercial break

with a message about how

robots are smart and useful—featuring

Robert, of course.

"Meow!" Nina

Simone purred excitedly

as she jumped on top of the

news desk and pranced in

front of the camera.

Frankie looked down at her *Citizens'*

Press badge. She knew Mama would be proud of everything she'd done—from creating her own news show to helping her big sister. Frankie couldn't wait for Mama to return so the entire family could watch the recording together. And she couldn't wait to report on more news in the future.

Ding-dong! The doorbell rang. Frankie and Raven looked at each other. Maybe Papa wasn't making his spaghetti dinner after all.

"Pizza?" the sisters guessed excitedly.

Frankie ended her show with a smile. "This is Frankie McKnight signing off to go eat pizza with Papa, Raven, and my trusted news crew. But make sure to stay tuned for *Frankie and Friends*. I'll be reporting on more kids' news that you can use soon!"

UNDERSTANDING THE NEWS

BREAKING NEWS is an event that is happening in the moment. Journalists are often some of the first people at the scene to gather information and give updates to the public. **JOURNALISM** is the profession of writing for newspapers, magazines, or news websites. People who work in this profession are called *journalists*. And journalists who share the news on television are called *reporters*. Sometimes, journalists have to report on **HARD NEWS**, which is very serious news that can be upsetting or scary. It's also time sensitive, which means that it's information that people need to know either immediately or sooner rather than later. Hard news is usually important to people all over the world, not just to the people in one community.

Everyone has an **OPINION**—it is their view or belief about something. However, opinions are not facts. So even though everyone's opinion is important, journalists are required to share information that has been proven to be true when it comes to reporting the news.

Often, news is a **DEVELOPING STORY**, which means journalists are still gathering important facts and information. Journalists report on these types of news stories as they are happening.

A **BEAT** is a subject that a reporter covers. Some reporters may have just one beat to report on. Other reporters may have several.

A **FACT** is something that is known or that has been proven to be true. It is very important that journalists and reporters share news that includes facts. Otherwise, they might give people the wrong information or their opinion about something instead of what actually happened.

An **INTERVIEW** is when one person asks another person questions. The person who is asking the questions is called the *interviewer*. The person who is answering the questions is called the *interviewee*. Interviews can happen in person, over the phone, or on the computer. Sometimes, an interviewer may even send questions to an interviewee so they can write out their answers.

When a reporter asks a **CLOSED-ENDED QUESTION**, there are only a few options for how someone can respond. These options can be a simple "yes" or "no." Or the reporter may include more details in the options. But the person can only choose a response from the limited options that they are given.

Unlike a closed-ended question, when a reporter asks an **OPEN-ENDED QUESTION,** someone can respond however they decide. They can give a

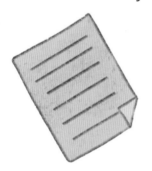

short response or a long response. They can even explain why they responded a certain way!

A **TAGLINE** is a short phrase that people can remember about who you are or the services you offer. It's usually very clever and unique!

About the Author

Christine Platt is an author and advocate who believes storytelling is a tool for social change. She holds a BA in Africana studies, an MA in African American studies, and a JD in general law. Although her only daughter is now in college, Christine Platt continues to draw on their adventures together as inspiration for her children's literature.

About the Illustrator

Alea Marley is an award-winning illustrator of many books for children, including *Phoebe Dupree Is Coming to Tea!* by Linda Ashman. She loves creating whimsical scenes that are filled with patterns, texture, and bursts of color. Alea Marley lives in northern England.

GO LIVE is a term used in journalism that means a reporter is about to start delivering the  news on the air. It also signals to everyone in the news studio or people who are near the reporter to be quiet. Otherwise, their voices will be heard when the reporter starts talking!